To Arthur (Dog) and Kitty (Cat)

• Little, Brown and Company • Hachette Book Group • 237 Park Avenue, New York, NY 10017 • Visit our website at www.lb-kids.com • Little, Brown and Company is a division of Hachette Book Group, Inc. • The Little, Brown name and logo are trademarks of Hachette Book Group, Inc. • The publisher is not responsible for websites (or their content) that are not owned by the publisher. • First Edition: May 2014 • Library of Congress Cataloging-in-Publication Data • Gall, Chris, author, illustrator. • Dog vs. Cat / Chris Gall. — First edition. • pages cm • Summary: A dog and a cat, both newly adopted and forced to share a room, do not get along until a howling, smelly, terrifying newcomer unites them in a common cause. • ISBN 978-0-316-23801-4 (hardcover) • [1. Dogs—Fiction. 2. Cats—Fiction. 3. Individuality—Fiction. 4. Friendship—Fiction.] I. Title. II. Title: Dog versus Cat. • PZ7.G1352Dog 2014 • [E]—dc23 • 2013015639 • 10 9 8 7 6 5 4 3 2 1 • SC • Printed in China

DOG vs. Cat

CHRIS GALL

LITTLE, BROWN AND COMPANY

New York   Boston

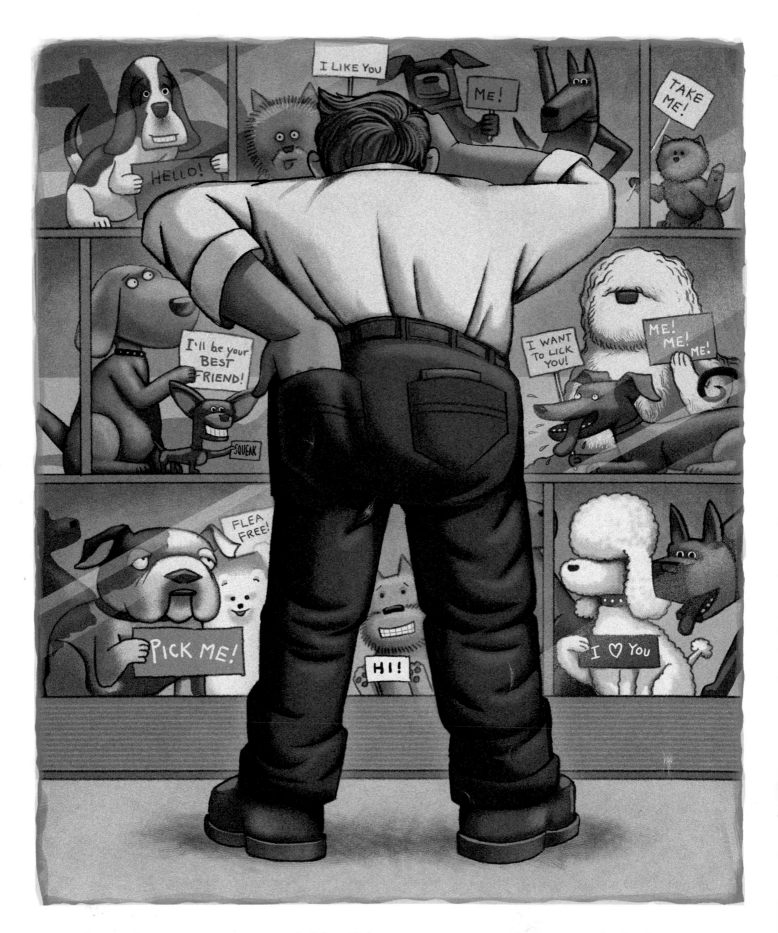

One day, a man named Mr. Button went to the animal shelter to pick out a friendly-looking dog.

Then he brought the dog home.

Across town, on that very same day, Mrs. Button went to a pet store and bought a smart-looking cat.

Then she brought the cat home.

However, the Buttons had only one room for their pets.
They would have to share.
This could have been a dangerous situation,
but Dog and Cat wanted to be very grown-up.

And so Dog and Cat moved in together.

Dog quickly arranged one side of the room.

Cat did the same with the other side.

Dog gave Cat a warm greeting, but Cat didn't like showers.

Cat offered Dog a "mousewarming" present.

Dog showed Cat how to chase a tail.

Cat showed Dog how to curl up with a good book.

Their habits were very different.

Dog liked to keep in touch with friends all day long.

Cat liked to play games all night long.

There were more problems.
Dog was always sniffing everything.

Cat would claw anything that moved.

And then there was the litter-box issue.

That was when they decided to mark their territories.

But neither Dog nor Cat was satisfied.

One of them had to go!

Cat knew that Dog had a very good nose.
So Cat made sure to maintain horrible garlic breath.

mmmm...

Dog rubbed some party balloons on the rug and stuck them to Cat.

Cat popped them with sharp claws, nearly giving Dog a heart attack.

Cat filled Dog's water bowl with hairballs.

Dog poured the water over
Cat's head during naptime.

IT WAS TOO MUCH TO TAKE!

Each pet was determined to get the other in trouble. Cat used a silent dog whistle to make Dog howl in the middle of the night.

Dog spread catnip over Mrs. Button's nice pillows so that Cat would go crazy. That was when the Buttons gave Dog and Cat a time-out.

Since they could agree on nothing else, Dog and Cat decided to build a wall to separate their room.

After they were finished, the room became very quiet. **TOO** quiet.

Soon, Dog began to remember all the good times they'd had together.

And Cat began to remember all the fun times, too.

They began to miss each other.

So Cat sent over a peace offering.

Dog replied.

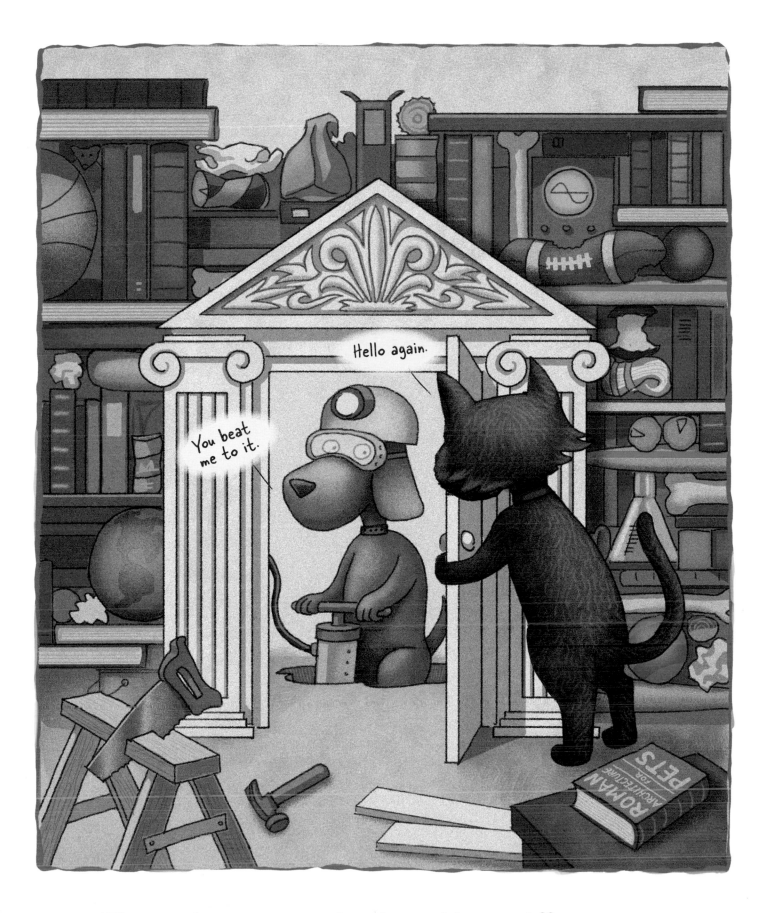

They each set out to solve the problem in different ways.

Then one day, Dog and Cat heard a strange howling outside their door.

Another pet! They could not believe that Mr. and Mrs. Button would wish for a pet any better than Dog or Cat.

What could it be?
Dog hoped it wasn't a porcupine.

Cat hoped it wasn't an elephant.

Dog and Cat were afraid. They agreed that something had to be done to keep the creature out of their room.

Cat drew up plans to block the door.

Dog tore down their wall and used the pieces.

But they forgot that the door opened into the hallway.

Then Mr. and Mrs. Button brought in the cage.

It was the most terrifying creature Dog and Cat had ever seen!

And it had moved into their bedroom!

The creature never
seemed to stop screeching.

And it certainly
couldn't use a litter box.

So Dog and Cat decided to move out.

But they knew of only one other available room.

Cat drew up the plans. Dog hammered nails and lifted the heavy things.

And when they were done, they shared a pitcher of cold lemonade.

The End